Alberto

Alberto

Adapted from The Velveteen Rabbit by Margery Williams

Words and Illustrations by John Jimerson

Coloring by Rose Jimerson and John Jimerson

Preliminary Line Art by Arnav Mazumdar and Danh Tran

To Rose, because you are you.

– Contents –

– Acknowledgments –

For their inspiring natures, good advice, financial support, and patience, or simply because they are gifts to the world, gratitude to these folks.

Margery Williams
Isla Rose Cassity
Mayer Levi Zitlin
Unity of the Triangle
Patricia A. Durmon
Neusom Holmes
Aric Rohner
Scott McKenzie
Salinger the cat
Denham Hardman
Allyson Van Gorder
R. Timothy Smith Jr.
Why Not Be Cheerful
Germain Choffart
Jory Castleberg
Nicola Bullock
Ursula Vernon
Barbara Park
Rose Jimerson
Charles Kochel
Andy Adams
Jennifer Alkove
Jimmy Durmon
The "Explorers" Class

The Little School
Jaybird Oberski
Phil Wilshire
John Monguillot
Jim Haverkamp
Margie James
PJ Maske
Haven Jimerson
River Bundy
Nam Holtz
Gregor McElvogue
Dana Marks
Jessica Flemming
Nancy Burns
Rich Kelleman
Curtis M. Plaza
Alice Turner
Johana Ramirez
Griego Martin Family
Alberto Rubio
Dan Daugherty
Jay Klinck
Jim Haverkamp
Joe Monaghan

Margie Carol
Nick Karner
Julie Morris
Saddler Hill Cooper
Leslie Tyndall
Garrett Jimerson
Alex Jimerson
Zach Jimerson
Patrick Ashlock
Patience
Rebecca Bossen
Meg Eighan
John Keener
River Bundy
Crystal Edler Schiller
Dimitrios Angelis
Randy Johnson
Dushyanth Surakanti
Mary Remmel Wohlleb
Trung Ngo
A Book Lover, California
Sylvia Tate
Sarah Jane Fenton
Ami Hudson

Brandon Hudson
Jane Holding
Birma Castle
David Jimerson
Starmaru
Brook North
Melissa K. Durmon
Ben Frink
Samantha Frink
Chad Bevins
Leo Ross Trevor
Carol Bryan
Kaleigh Bryan
Frank U. Jeffreys
Chris Barr
Maria Leblanc
Tanya Vacharkulksemsuk
Ann Laser
Kissane Myer Family
Lily Grace Stallings
Nicole Stone
Amy Allen
Cindy Long Ragsdale

– Chapter 1 –

Arrival

Once, there was a rabbit.

He arrived in a stocking one morning, and oh my goodness, he was cute.

A little boy hugged him tight and ran through the house singing "This is my bunny! His name is Alberto! I love him — Alberto Alberto Alberto!"

And they played...

and they built alphabets...

and they flew with capes.

A few days later, the Christmas things were put away, and in the midst of all the cleaning...

the rabbit was misplaced.

And the boy couldn't find him.

– Chapter 2 –

Na-Na and a Horse

Na-Na was the big-time cleaner-upper of toys.

To the toys, she was a tornado. She would SWOOP down, snatch them up, and drop them into boxes and onto shelves.

The toys all hated it, especially the hard ones.

OOF!

But Alberto didn't mind because his bottom was fluffy.

(Poof!)

Alberto spent most of his time listening to loud electric toys who all bragged about how **real** they were.

The boat bragged about discovering **real** pirate treasure. The cars claimed they raced in **real** drag races, and the robot thumped his chest and said he discovered a **real** alien planet!

But the rabbit didn't brag about anything. He didn't even know real rabbits existed.

He thought other rabbits were like him: velveteen fur, button eyes, and stuffed with sawdust.

It got lonesome around so many braggers.

Then, one day, Alberto met a horse.

The horse was much older than the other toys. He had been loved for years by the boy, and before him, by the boy's uncle when he was a boy, and before him, by the boy's uncle's mother, when she was a girl. As a result, the horse looked more like a clump of dirt than a horse. His wheels didn't work, most of his tail hair was missing, and all over his body, there were pictures of starfish and seashells drawn by kids.

Also, he knew a secret:

"Most toys always stay toys," said the horse. "Even if they brag, they don't usually become real."

"What is real?"

"Real isn't how you are made," explained the horse. "When a kid loves you for a long, long time, not just to play with, but really loves you, then you become real."

"Does it hurt?"

"Sometimes, but when you are real, you don't mind being hurt."

Does it happen slowly, or all at once?

It takes a long time. That's why it doesn't happen to toys who have sharp edges or who have to be carefully kept. By the time you are real, most of your hair has been loved off, and your eyes drop out, and your stains have stains. But these things don't matter, because once you are real, you are not ugly ... except maybe to those who don't understand.

Are you real?

Yes. I became real to the boy's uncle years and years ago. Once you become real to a child, you can't become un-real again. It lasts for always.

"**I want to be real too!**" said the rabbit. "But I don't want stains and hair loss. Maybe if I'm careful..."

Just then, Na-Na swooped Alberto up, shoved him into the boy's arms, and said...

I can't find your floppy dog for bedtime. Here-take-your-rabbit-he's-floppy-like-a-dog.

Alberto! Where have you been?

Toy box. Also the floor.

Then it was bedtime.

Sleeping in the bed took lots of patience at first. You may not know this, but sleeping is hard when someone is laying on top of your head.

It's harder when they drool.

But eventually, these two figured it out.

– Chapter 3 –

Left Outside

The boy and the bunny played so much that Alberto's fur was getting worn out, and his tail was coming off, but he didn't notice. It was spring time, and the two of them played outside every day.

One day, the boy was called in for snacks, and he ran off so fast that he left Alberto outside by mistake.

t grew darker. The stars came out. Na-Na rushed across the lawn with
a flashlight and grumbled to herself about rabbits and why in the world
didn't she go to law school.

She found the rabbit, wiped him off on her blouse, and hurried to the boy's room. "Why are you throwing such a fit over this dirty toy?" she said.

"Na-Na," the boy said firmly, "that isn't nice manners." Na-Na's eyes opened wide. "He **isn't** a toy to me — he's **REAL!**"

Alberto heard this, and he couldn't believe it. After so much wishing, he was **REAL**!

That night, he was so happy that he couldn't sleep, and the next morning he felt different somehow.

Even Na-Na noticed the difference and said "That rabbit looks like he's up to something."

– Chapter 4 –

Bunny Tag

A few weeks later, the boy took Alberto outside and made a nest of grass for him in the backyard. Then he ran off to play with some friends.

Alberto was sitting in his nest watching ants play follow the leader, and he heard something move behind the ferns.

Then, that something jumped over the ferns and landed right next to him! It was two somethings! They were **rabbits**! They looked brand new! He didn't see any seams or threads or anything. He couldn't see their on/off switches, but they moved like magic. One minute, they were long and thin, and the next minute, they were fat and bunchy.

They stared at him. He stared back.
Everyone's noses twitched.

"Hiya!" said the gray rabbit. "We're playing bunny tag. Wanna play with us?"

"Um ... I don't feel like it?"

Alberto knew he was real to the boy, but he was still a toy. So, he didn't want to talk about his sawdust stuffing and the "no batteries" situation.

"Doop dee doo! Come on — it's super easy! I dare you. Plus, I don't think you can!" The rabbit hopped sideways then stood straight up.

"I can! I can jump higher than you!" said Alberto.

(He meant when the boy threw him, but he didn't want to say so.)

Can you hop on your
hind legs?" asked the
rabbit, as he jumped into
the air.

"Ummm..." said Alberto.

Fun fact: Alberto had no
hind legs. All he had
down there was a back
and a front and a squishy
bottom. So, he sat still,
and he hoped the other
rabbits wouldn't notice.

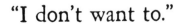

"I don't want to."

Wild rabbits have very sharp eyes, and the brown one stretched out his neck and looked.

"He hasn't got any hind legs!" he called out to his friend. "What happened to you!?! It's HORRIBLE!"

Then he laughed. "You're a ... ha ha ... rabbit ... Ha Ha ... without LEGS! HA HA HAHAHAHA!"

Then he and his friend laughed so hard they fell over.

"I do so have legs!" Alberto said quickly. "I am sitting on them!"

"Then stretch them out and show me, like this!" said the gray rabbit, and he whirled around and danced.

"I don't like dancing," said Alberto. "I'd rather sit still." But inside him, he wanted to play.

The wild rabbit stopped moving and leaned in close to Alberto's face. His long whiskers brushed the toy rabbit's ear. Then, he wrinkled his nose, and he jumped backwards.

"He smells funny!" the rabbit exclaimed. "He isn't real!"

"I am real to the **boy**," said Alberto. "The boy said I was real!"

He was very confused. He felt like he should be able to play with them, but he didn't know how. Then the boy appeared, and the wild rabbits ran. They jumped through the fence and disappeared into the woods.

They were gone.

– Intermission –

You made it to the intermission!

Plays and musicals often have intermissions, but not books.
But this **book** has an intermission!

During an intermission, everyone takes a little break.
You can stretch, or get a drink of water,
or even go to sleep.

When you're ready to read again,
just open the book to this page,
and keep going.

Enjoy your intermission!

(By the way, great job. You just read half of a chapter book!)

– Chapter 5 –

Feeling Sick

Weeks and weeks passed. Alberto and the boy had so much fun that Alberto looked like a very dirty lump. He didn't even look like a rabbit anymore, except to the boy. To him, the rabbit was always perfect.

Then one day, the boy became sick - very sick.

Have you ever been so sick that you couldn't move? That's how sick the boy was. The doctors didn't know how to fix this kind of sick. So, the boy stayed in bed, and his family hoped that he would get better. The rabbit stayed close to the boy and hid under the covers so no one would take him. He knew the boy needed him.

The boy was too sick to even read. So, Alberto whispered stories into
his ear about all the fun they would have when he got better: running
and hopping and playing outside! Maybe the boy could even get another
rabbit, and they could all play together.

Finally, the boy's fever broke, and for the first time in a long time, he got out of bed and went for a short walk outside.

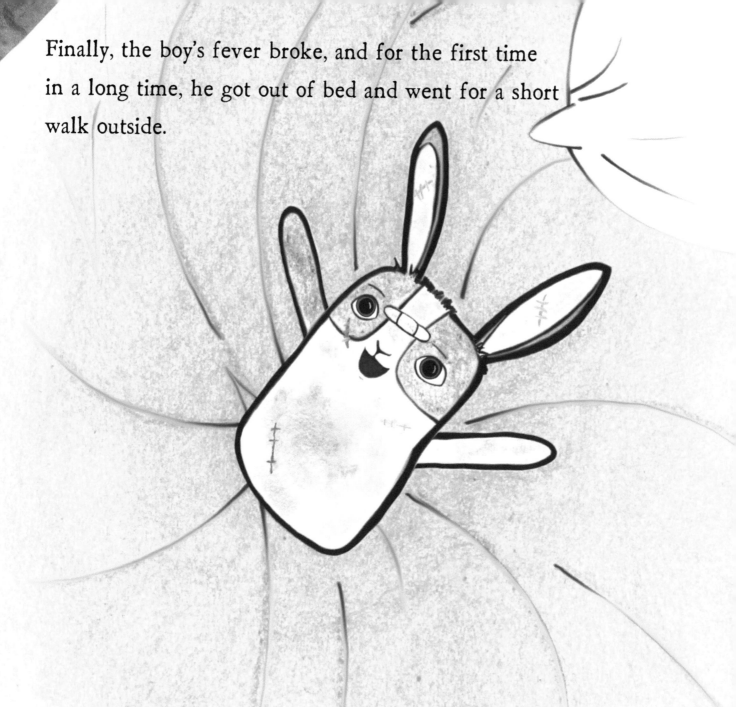

It was a bright sunny day, and Alberto lay there daydreaming.

He overheard the grown-ups talking about a trip to the ocean! The bedroom was to be cleaned, and everything with germs was to be thrown away. "We're going to the ocean!" he thought.

I love the ocean! Well, I've never been there, but it sounds amazing! There are crabs. You can build sandcastles! You can dig in the sand and cover your whole self up except for your face! It's like a never-ending supply of dirt! Except it's sand. I LOVE DIRT.

Have you ever been? I'm going to put on sunglasses ... then, I'm going to put on sunscreen ... then ... do you think they'll let me go snorkeling?
That's a weird word.
Snorkel... snorkel... snorkel...

Na-Na saw the rabbit in the bed and asked "What about that old bunny?"

The doctor said "Oh no. Everything in the bed goes into the trash. It's full of germs."

And before Alberto knew what happened...

Na-Na

made

one

last ...

swoop.

43

She put Alberto, the sheets, and the other bed things into a garbage bag and she carried them outside. The boy's father would burn them tomorrow morning.

That night, the boy fell asleep in the living room after watching his favorite show. So, he didn't even notice that Alberto was gone.

– Chapter 7 –

A Visitor

Alberto was cold, and he felt lonely
The bag came untied; so, he stuck
his little head out to see what he
could see.

He saw the place where the boy made nests for
him and where he met the other rabbits. He
remembered being thrown into the air and talking
with his friend the horse.

"What good is it?" Alberto thought. "Why even try? Why try to become real, if this is how it ends?"

And a tear, a REAL tear, trickled down his little velvet nose and fell to the ground.

Then a strange thing happened.

In the **exact** spot where the tear hit the ground, a flower burst out of the earth.

It glowed, and it was unlike any other flower in the backyard that night.

As it grew towards him, Alberto thought he heard faraway music, and the green leaves sparkled light on everything around them.

At the center of the leaves was a bright golden cup that opened its petals, releasing sad but joy-filled music into the quiet night.

And out of the flower stepped ...

a fairy.

She was soulful this fairy.

When she spoke, she sang. And she sang the blues.

"Little rabbit...," she sang. "Little Raaaaaaaa-bit!" "Little raaaaaaaabbit..."
Then faster: "Do – You – Know – Who – I – AAAAAAAAM?"

Hiding his face with the trash bag, the rabbit screeched "I don't!
You're scary! Why are you singing your talking?"

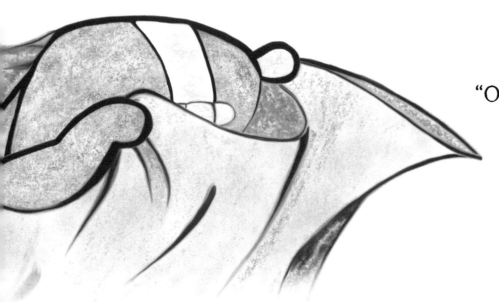

"Oh! Sorry about that.
Take ten, boys!"
she commanded,
and the music
stopped.

"Honey," she said softly, flying to Alberto, "you seem to be in a pickle."

The rabbit was very confused.

I am not a "honey," and I am not "in a pickle." I am a rabbit. And I am in a trash bag. They may burn me up tomorrow.

That sounds awful.

I agree...
Who are you?

Name's Dinah. I'm the fairy of toy magic. I take care of toys that children have loved on, and help turn them into real.

I wasn't real before?

You were real, to the **boy**, because he loved you," said the fairy. "Now, you'll be real to **everybody**."

Then she held him close and lifted him into the air.

Be careful!" he squeaked. Please be CAREFUL!"

You're safe, bunny," she said.

53

Together they flew into the woods, leaving behind them a sparkling blue trail that sounded faintly like guitars and harmonicas.

Chapter 8

Time to Dance

Wild rabbits were dancing on soft grass in the moonlight, and when they saw the fairy, they stopped and stood in a circle staring at her.

"Hey fun bunnies," said the fairy.

"I brought you a new friend. Will you be kind to him?"

The rabbits nodded.

"Will you teach him everything he needs to know here in Rabbit-land?"

They nodded again. Then, she gave Alberto a kiss on the top of his head and put him down on the grass. "Welcome to your new bunny-home," she said. "You can run and play now."

But he just sat there.

He saw all the wild rabbits and remembered that he couldn't jump. He didn't want them to laugh at him again.

Then something tickled his nose, and he lifted his hind toe to scratch it.

wait

 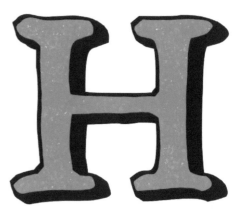

A T ?

He had a hind TOE!

. . . . His ear

REAL

A

REAL

REAL FUR!

HE WAS

nd hind leg had

60

. . . It was connected to a HIND LEG! . . . His toe twitched, and he had real whiskers! . . .

RABBIT!

When the fairy kissed him, she gave him the last magical nudge he needed, and he transformed.

Sometimes that's how things happen.

61

He **leapt** into the air, and he hopped forward and backward and side to side to test out these amazing new things. He even did a handstand and wiggled his new feet in the breeze.

When he finally stopped to thank the fairy, she was gone.

Alberto was real.

He was finally a real rabbit, at home with other rabbits.

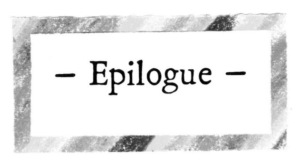

– Epilogue –

Autumn passed, and winter too, and during all that time, the boy looked for Alberto but couldn't find him. In the spring, when it grew warmer, the boy was playing outside. Two rabbits hopped into the yard and stared at him. No one moved.

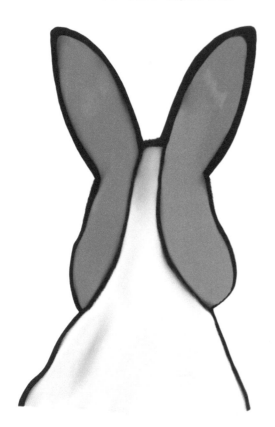

One rabbit had strange markings on his fur that looked a lot like stitching, and the boy thought there was something familiar about those eyes.

Hello bunny," he said, putting his hand out. "You look just like my old bunny, Alberto, who got lost when I was sick."

The rabbit put his nose on the boy's hand, then looked up at him, as if he wanted to say something. What do you imagine he might have wanted to say?

The rabbits came back every now and then, but the boy never knew that one of them was Alberto, who kept coming back to play with the boy who helped him to be Real.

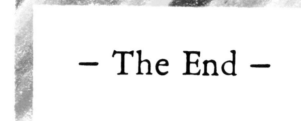

- The End -

CPSIA information can be obtained
at www.ICGtesting.com
Printed in the USA
LVHW071130160821
695401LV00002B/71